Marian Ivens

Tyrone Alone

AuthorHouse™ UK
1663 Liberty Drive
Bloomington, IN 47403 USA
www.authorhouse.co.uk
UK TFN: 0800 0148641 (Toll Free inside the UK)
UK Local: 02036 956322 (+44 20 3695 6322 from outside the UK)

This book is printed on acid-free paper.

ISBN: 978-1-6655-8952-9 (sc)
978-1-6655-8951-2 (e)

Print information available on the last page.

Published by AuthorHouse 06/03/2021

authorHOUSE®

Tyrone Alone

"Be a good boy! On your bed! Back soon!"

"She's gone! That was the front door shutting!"

Tyrone jumped quickly from his bed and peered out of the window, his paws on the window sill.

"Must be Math's Monday. Marcie always carries that bag with all those funny squiggles on it, when it's Monday."

"Mmmmmm, free until lunchtime!"

Tyrone pointed his nose in the air and sniffed. Marcie has forgotten to take her snack, those crunchy biscuits, the ones she baked last night.

"She didn't give me much of a taste!" he sniffed grumpily. "She won't notice if I sample some more!"

HOME
SWEET
HOME

Tyrone padded intro the kitchen. On the worktop there was the biscuit tub, the ones you can see inside, and there were the crunchy biscuits.

"My favourite!" Tyrone licked his lips.

He raised his nose as high as he could towards the edge of the worktop, but, no matter how much he stretched his neck and nose he could not reach the tub.

"Grrrr....well, nothing else for it, I will have to jump up," he decided.

The worktop was quite high for a little dog, but Tyrone had done this before! Marcie had never caught him, but she had started to wonder how few biscuits there always seemed to be in the biscuit tub.

TYRONE

Tyrone poked his nose under one foot of the kitchen chair and pushed; then he poked his nose under another foot and pushed.

"Nearly there, one more push! Ah, there, good, right against the side of the worktop. Works every time!" he grinned.

And quick as a flash, up he jumped from floor to the chair to the worktop.

"Now how did I do this last time? Ah, yes, there's one loose corner. Got it!"

The lid came off very quickly in his sharp little teeth, and the biscuits disappeared quickly too!

TYRONE

From the top of the worktop there was a good view of the kitchen and the garden outside through the window.

The washing up was all done and there were some flowers in the kitchen window. As he looked, from the corner of this eye he saw Duchess, the neighbour's cat lazily strolling across the garden.

Tyrone leapt off the worktop to the window, knocking the flowers onto the floor where the water puddled and trickled under the cooker.

"Woof! Woof! Woof! Woof! Cheeky cat! Out of my garden! Out, I say!!"

Duchess raised her beautiful green eyes and curled her shiny white tail. "What a silly dog," she said to herself. "As if I care about his noisy barking!" And she stared boldly, straight at Tyrone.

"Woooooof! Wooooooooof! Bossy cat! Who does she think she is! Grrrrrr!"

Duchess continued her lazy walk, then effortlessly leapt to the top of the garden wall where she lay preening herself in the sunshine.

Tyrone barked louder and louder. He scraped his claws wildly on the glass, but, Duchess just looked the other way.

He was so put out that when he spied Marcie's slippers peeking out from under the sitting room chair, in a trice, they were in his mouth. He shook and shook and shook until the silky fur was floating in the air like snowflakes.

"Ahhhhh…… I feel better after that!" he panted happily. "That snooty cat always annoys me!"

But when he saw the lovely white fur on the carpet, well, he just couldn't stop himself from rolling and wriggling in it.

"Ah……. that feels good! Got a tickly bit in the middle of my back….. mmmmm, perfect! That's the spot."

And so he rolled, all four legs in the air, wriggling and scratching and ahhhing!

Finally, when the fur started to tickle his nose and he had "Aitishoooed!" several time he decided he had enough and chewed the juicy, rubbery rest of the slipper into little bits.

Suddenly, the clock in the hall cuckooed eleven o'clock.

The cuckoo popped in and out, in and out. Tyrone barked and put his dirty paws on the wall, annoyed he could not reach that irritating bird!

He jumped, and jumped and jumped up. He snapped his teeth but the bird took no notice!!

Cuckoo – Jump, Cuckoo – Jump, Cuckoo – Jump, Cuckoo – Jump.....!

Up and down! Up and down! Up and down!

Eleven times. And stop. Tyrone flopped to the floor and rolled over, all four legs in the air. "Bother, I'll get you one day, you silly bird!"

"Oooh, Marcie'll be back in an hour. Hope she has remembered I wanted a new chewy bone.

Bang! Bang! Bang!

“What was that?” Tyrone pricked up his ears and followed the sound.” Bang! Bang! Bang!

Marcie had forgotten to lock the back door and it was banging backwards and forwards in a sharp little breeze.

Tyrone bounded outside, hoping Duchess was still on the wall, but no, Duchess, in disgust, had left her sunbathing. What a disappointment; he really wanted to chase that cat!

Tyrone mooched around the garden.

"Now, I am sure there's a tennis ball or two out here!"

He sniffed about; behind the wheelie bin, under the garden seat, under the pile of empty plant pots, behind the back door. He lifted his head for a second. The sharp little breeze was whipping the washing round on the whirligig really fast.

The legs of Marcie's blue pyjamas were flapping madly and spinning round and round.

"What fun!"

Tyrone galloped over to the whirligig and grabbed a pyjama leg in his mouth. He ran round and round, gripping it tightly in his sharp, white teeth. His feet left the ground!

"Wheeeeeee! This is marvelous fun! Wheeeee!"

Round and round, swing, swing, swiiiiiing, until scrrrrrrch – oh dear, the pyjama leg had ripped! Tyrone was jolted to a standstill with a piece of blue pyjama leg in his mouth.

"Uh…oh! Well, that's that! What a pity! It was a great game!" he panted.

Need a drink after all that swinging about. "Mmmmmmm! I wonder?"

Tyrone prodded his nose against the back door and padded into the kitchen. He ran his nose up the side of the fridge door and………, wiggle, wiggle, wiggle and there, the door was open.

"Milk, now where is it? In the door."

Carefully, carefully Tyrone placed his mouth around the narrow top of the milk bottle and lifted it out of the fridge door. It was quite heavy, but, as he had done this before, he knew he had to be very gentle. He sat the bottle on the floor and pressed his nose into the foil top.

"Just a little hole, that's it. Easy to tear now!"

"Now where is my bowl?"

Tyrone nosed his dog bowl to the side of the milk bottle and tipped the bottle so the milk – well some of it – went into the bowl. The rest puddled on to the floor.

Lap, lap, lap, lap – ooh, delicious.

BREAD

MILK
TYRONE

Of course, when Tyrone trotted into the sitting room, he left a trail of white, wet paw prints behind him.

"Must be time for a nap," he said to himself. "But first I will check what's on the TV."

He nosed underneath the cushions and sure enough, there was the remote. He tipped it on to the floor with a flick of his front paw and pressed a button.

"Hooray it's Cats World."

Tyrone eagerly stared at the cats on the TV. He barked. He pawed at the screen. He jumped on and off the settee in his excitement and whined jealousy at the delicious food that those spoiled cats were fed!

Now it really did feel like time for a nap.

He spied the ironing basket full of some very comfortable looking blouses and pillow cases and smelling sweetly from drying in the sunshine.

"Oh, yes, just right."

And he snuggled down deep into the clean clothes and intro a contented, snuffly sleep.

TY
NE

"Hello! I am home! Have you been a good boy?"

Marcie put down her bags.

"Well, Tyrone," she said. "You have been busy!"

Printed in the United States
by Baker & Taylor Publisher Services